MONISHA BATRA

ISBN 979-8-88909-958-1

CONTENTS

PREFACE

Dear Reader!

Thank you for picking this up and deciding to climb *the Eighteen Steps* by giving it a read.

Oftentimes, I have been told by my family, friends, acquaintances, and colleagues how thought-provoking my poetry pieces are. I want to thank each person I've met in this journey of life for filling my pot of experiential learning and knowledge. This includes all those who have shared their personal experiences, it is never easy to let out the most vulnerable side of yours in front of someone, but once we do, we are already in a much better place than before. Kudos to you for being able to do that.

I started writing in the year 1998, and it has been such an enriching journey so far.

When I started writing this book, I never imagined that one day I would be penning what you are reading right now. Each day while writing 'The Eighteen Steps,' goosebumps and unexplainable excitement have been the constants.

The Eighteen Steps is a 'Fraction' – blending fiction and non-fiction in a poetic way. This is a poetic voyage of a girl 'Amanda' and her experiences described over a span of Eighteen Steps.

This 'Poetic Voyage' is Amanda's life story described through a collection of self-written Poetry pieces intertwined with her life expeditions in the story.

A combination of Narrative, Rhymed, and Free Verse Poetry, each poem absorbs the sentiments of Amanda as she travels through each phase in her life and takes another step from the start till the Eighteenth one.

This book has the unconditional wishes, efforts, and support of *my parents - Mrs Molina and Mr Ajay Batra,* who made me envision myself as an author early in life and nurtured the thought all through. You have been my best cheerleaders and critics, making me strive to become a better version of myself every day. This book wouldn't have been possible without you.

I would like to thank my friend, the illustrator and editor of this book, *who prefers to be Unnamed till my readers make me 'reach the speech' at Harvard,* for adding splashes of vibrancy through his creative illustrations and suggestive editing.

The 1st

START-OUT

In the heart of India, embracing the journey called 'Life,' Amanda was born to a family where her birth was celebrated upon frills and fanfare. Her parents were elated, thankful to the Almighty and in celebratory mode.

Celebrating small achievements, learning cycling, seeing the helium balloons go up in the sky so high, and enjoying her favourite flavour of ice cream, life was full of simple joys for her. Sparkling eyes, radiant smiles, and contagious laughter made the environment exhilarating.

The chapters of life gradually unfold by narrating experiences, opening new challenges, and bringing in fresh rays of hope.

Years passed...

"School, examinations, friends, family, weekly tests, so much to do!" thought Amanda.

This journey isn't easy, but what learning each day.

And,

Before she realised it, it was 'Summer Vacation' time! And Summer vacation meant homework and vacation with friends and family.

Vacationing with family at the Andamans this time during the summer vacations, the beauty of the place overpowers the senses and mesmerises the core.

The waves hug the feet momentarily, and then the sand again dominates the shore.

Sitting by the beach one day, she described the chapter of life in her own way ...

A Chapter Of Life

A cup of warm tea,
The humming of the bees,
The rustle of the dry leaves,
The subtle waving of the branches of the trees.

Watching the sun go down,
We -- portraying the role of a real-life clown,
A moment of laughter, another frown,
The hope's safety gear, averting the drown.

Solo walk on a moonlit night,
Stargazing, the subliminal thoughts taking over the mind,
The silence conveys the message, untold,
The soul, waiting for the story to unfold.

The fragrance of the flowers, the vibrant hues of the sky,
Listening to the notes enchanted by the birds
as they fly.

A new today, inhibitions at bay,
A little sway, an attempt to explore the unexplored way!

The 2ⁿᵈ

LIFE'S RACE

'Amanda,' a daydreamer, an observer, star gazing at night, started reflecting upon life as the years passed. The clouds played hide and seek with the stars, yet the stars continued to twinkle. She started resonating with the experiences in life and how an attempt to overcome the odds makes us see the light at the end of the tunnel.

Thoughts merged in the darkness of the night, self-introspective discussions pacified and gave way to the first ray of Sunshine.

Amanda headed to her school just like another usual weekday.

In the middle of a busy day at school, sitting by the basketball field, thoughts racing on the dirt track of experiences, she imagined herself sitting in the corner of a crossroad. The imaginary self, aspiring to reach the pinnacle, the rush, the commotion, the celebration, and the introspection.

Numbness creeping in, her brain's pulley came to a temporary halt.

While heading back home, seated right at the farthest end of the bus, Amanda started penning down her thoughts.

The Other Side of the Street

I sat in a corner,
Attempting to decode the vaguely familiar genre..
Commotion on one side,
Poker faces hiding a tide of turmoil inside..

Rushing to avoid missing the flight,
Expectations explode into a frivolous fight..

Celebratory meets to coffee dates,
Merely 86,000 seconds and so much to introspect..

Joyous, perplexed, anxious, numb,
A sea of emotions reciting a new hymn..
But ever wondered, the lyrics still remained the same!

And here I was,
Trying to read the text through the blotted spots,
Re-stacking the puzzle, re-joining the dots..

Alternating the pace of the stride,
The disoriented thoughts locked in the locker, which
read 'access denied'..

The subconscious foot tapping to the life's uniquely
presented symphony,
Made me contemplate if this was always the unexplored
me?

Walking through the labyrinth determined to succeed,
I confidently crossed to the other side of the street!

The 3rd

TRAVELLER

Exploring new vistas, the 'Wanderer' in her travelled. Travelled across the country and the globe in search of new experiences, new insights widening the spectrum and watching reality through the traveller's lens.

Backpacking along the journey of life, the 'traveller girl' was all set to explore the unexplored and soak in the mystery of the unknown and, this time to a beach town in the Southern part of India.

Each place has its own essence. Amanda was a firm believer in experiencing the journey in its entirety than the destination itself. The warmth of the Sun, the fragrance of the wet mud, the smiling faces zipping through the eye view, and the heart overwhelmed by the conversation of a few is always an amalgamation of the picturesque sightseeing and soaking in the essence of the cultures.

As she travelled through cities and towns, she was struck with sonder. Every few hours, she halted for a break and could not help but ponder as moments lapsed in front of her eyes, how different each person's journey is. How the Wanderer in each is nothing but the explorer in them.

Traveller

Coffee and Cookies,
The buzzing of the bees,
The highway, the sky, the hills, and the trees..
The surrendering of self to the purity of the breeze..

Driving through the cities and states,
On roads soaked in the rain..

Inching towards the destination,
The cheerful grin depicting the level of elation..

The sight of the coconut plantations,
The birds singing the 'oh-so-familiar rendition..

The waves, peaceful but powerful lashing the shore,
The unexpected thunder knocking the sky's door..

The water and the land,
Clasping each other's hands..
The feet sinking into the sand,
A step towards the water, a push back towards the land..

The tides soaking the soul,
Mesmerized, I stood numb, blank along the shore..

The mind moved away from doing its daily chore,
Serenity – a natural cure!
Surfing through the waves of ideas in store,
I barely started walking away, and the soul shouted –
encore!

The 4th

STRUGGLE

manda, walking on the pebbled path in the courtyard, reading her favourite book, thinking about her upcoming examinations, wondered about the essence of life.

'What if the results of my examinations do not come as expected?' she thought.

The contemplative Amanda sat in the corner of the room, worrying about contingencies. Little did she realise that she was paving the way for inhibitions to take over the cerebral space.

Minutes later, still in a state of bewilderment, she pulled out pages from her diary and started to read what she had once scribbled.

She recalled her last trip to the beaches and got reminded of the day when she sat on the rocks while watching the tides lash the shore, despite the rocks attempting to slow down the pace.

'Aspirations to reach the pinnacle may be similar, but all of us have a different path towards it,' she realised.

Opening the same diary she was reading a few hours back, she started scribbling her most recent experience with self-introspection.

STOP
STOP
STOP
STOP
STOP

The 'what if' overpowering the 'it will be okay'..
The contingent thought of the result while setting the
wet clay.

Directionless, she roamed..
Thinking faculties zoned.

The outcome out of sight..
Left her bewildered in the state of plight.
Closing her eyes for a while..
Rekindling the dusty notes labelled "intuition" on the
cover of the file.

Recalling the way the mother hugs the child..
Whether the room is in darkness or bright light.

She boarded that flight..
The route to the destination, which she herself did
decide.

The fire and warrior spirit to survive..
The life jacket on, yet the urge to dive.

It is sometimes not about the road less or
more often travelled.
Baffled?
Instead, it is about the road you want to travel on.
It is about carving the path you want to walk on.

Imperfections are natural,
Authenticity is their best collateral.

Sometimes awkward but real..
We are humans, and isn't this ideal?

'You need to reach the pinnacle'
Often times sounds biblical.
The thought of the view from the top of the pyramid
sounds magical..
The imaginative characters are theatrical.

The trek up there has its highs and lows..
But isn't that how the stream flows?
At times, till the knee, sometimes the toes..
Before the river welcomes it by opening its doors.

The 5th

FLUTTER

Through the years, as she grew up, ups and downs became a usual course.

The anxiety of examination results, college admissions, fearing failures, and celebrating moments of success…. All in a bouquet.

From 'Let me see the newspaper, the cut-off percentages will be out today' to 'I finally made it to the college of my choice.' The journey for Amanda had indeed been a rollercoaster one.

'What shall I be wearing' to 'What can I expect in college on Day 1?' the thoughts running amok, seldom contradicting each other, other times complementing.

From momentary celebrations to unforeseen disappointments, these rollercoaster rides were now a part of Amanda's life. She began to understand how important it was for her to start trusting her own self, shun away inhibitions and follow her intuitive self.

The bird in her had to open her wings, flutter and fly even with broken wings.

You can fly even with broken wings,
Untangling the knotted strings.

The Sun hiding behind the blanket of clouds,
The result before the relentless efforts bowed.

Not always a freeway, sometimes a pebbled path,
The room of aspirations filled with paper darts.

The trial and error, efforts encore,
The joy of exploring sea shells on the side of the shore.

Never abandon yourself when low,
You are the master of your own show!

A flight boarded alone,
Inhibitions dethroned.

Coz,
Dreams don't come true,
If you don't trust 'YOU'..

The 6th

PUZZLED THOUGHTS

The college days – the classes, the fest, and participating in plays.

From 'Wow, now college life begins' to 'I am in my final year of graduation. Shall I focus on my masters? or shall I sit for campus placements and start working?' Amanda's mind began to contemplate.

Weighing the pros and cons, measuring the risk appetite, and seeking advice from others, her cerebral cells made Venn diagrams to analyse and enable decision-making.

The risk of stumbling remains in every action; however, there is the light of hope after the darkness of numbness.

Standing at the crossroad, she wondered, 'Is it always about the road less travelled or the road we wish to travel on?'

The unknown artist blends the tints of blue..
Oh, those hues!!!
I wonder..

As the hours passed, events started to unfold..
The envelope opened, the letters dancing, conveying the
story untold..

Pitch dark night and..
..that one star sneaking its way through and twinkling
bright..
The drone of hope wandered over the gloomy skies..
The little birdie attempting to flutter, take its first flight
and rise!

A rough terrain,
A narrow lane,
Being behind the wheel,
"Skimming mentally through contingency plans the
brain cells wandered..

Though not a board of caution in sight, the hopeful
self wondered..
Wondered about the impeccable ways in which
aspiration and inspiration are soldered..
The anxiety and achievement eventually bartered.

Abounding aspirations..
Decoding the unexplained notations..
The peaceful sight of the blooming carnations..
A flash of reaching the destination and that
instantaneous feeling of elation.

In the end,
Goals, near or far..
The road- pebbled or tarred..
The journey, sometimes smooth other times scarred.
The constant wish from the shooting star..
Watching the bud blossom into a beautiful flower.

While I wander in the arena of my subliminal
thoughts,
I wonder about the beauty with which life's chapters are
tied through experiential knots,

I wander while I wonder!

The 7th

TRANSFORMATION

The preparation started - Mock interviews, aptitude tests, and grooming.

The path, once blurry, began to be vividly visible as the date of the actual interviews got nearer.

Rounds of nerve-racking interviews, moments wrapped in layers of anxiety, followed by a sigh of relief!

Amanda was now at a place she envisioned herself to be.

August 6, 2012

Day 1 (at work)

As she stepped in on her first day at work, a plethora of emotions took over.

Excitement

Anxiety

Nervousness

Confidence

Hope

Inner belief

Phew! What an avalanche of emotions.

She sat at her desk, determined to embark on this new journey.

However, at this onset, she decided to write a note reminding herself of what she is and what she aspires to be.

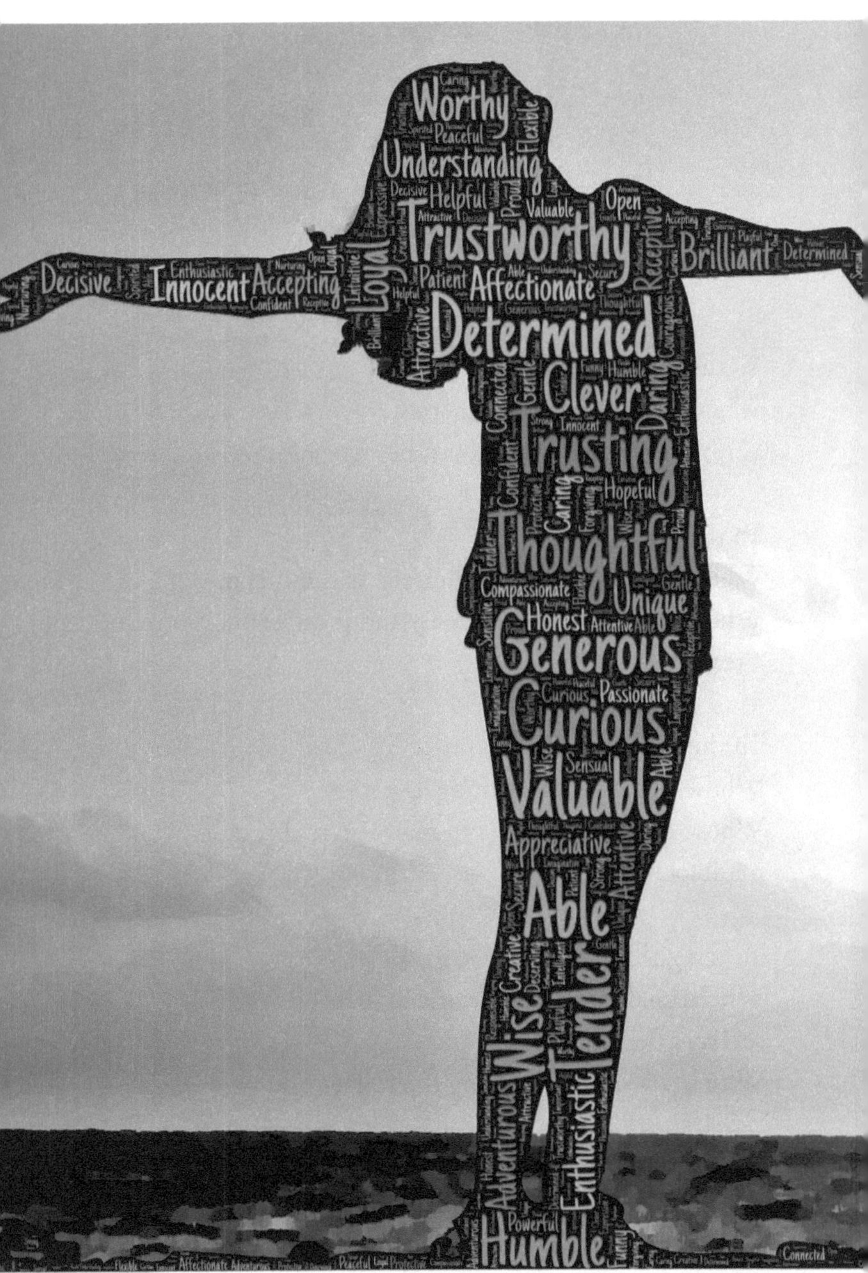

To the girl,
Who loves to chase her dreams,
With every accomplishment, her face beamed.

To the girl,
Who is unapologetically 'herself' without fear,
Who fights out the miseries without the explicit trace of
a tear?

To the girl,
Whose principles are strong as a rock,
Whose favourite drive is to manoeuvre through
roadblocks.

To the girl,
Whose goals are more futuristic than
society's beliefs,
Who has a smile observing the foliage and new leaves.

To the girl,
Whose beauty is defined by her soul, so pure,
A soul to which shallow attractions hold no allure.

To the girl,
Who reads through the silence..
Who finds the direction through superfluous presence.

You are..
The hope for many who struggle to think..
The confidence-loaded favourite drink..
The reflection of the dream, which has a reality check..
The determination needed to complete that unknown
rough terrain trek.

Believing in yourself isn't a virtue but the truth,
Dodgy and blinding, but the correct route.
Whenever in self-doubt,
"You are worth it!" Shout it back to yourself, and this
time around, say it aloud!

The 8th

TEAR

February 6, 2013

Amanda completed six months of her professional journey and wondered, 'What a rollercoaster ride it has been! Sometimes ecstatic, other times anxiety stricken.'

From understanding work to knowing colleagues, from stumbling while performing her tasks to being recognised through rewards, it had indeed been an experienced-soaked journey for Amanda.

As the journey's reel re-winded and replayed in front of her eyes, a tear rolled down her cheek, falling on the pillowcase.

A single tear silently embedding countless emotions, the calmness and the high tides, the smooth roads and the bumpy rides, the celebratory and the blurry days.

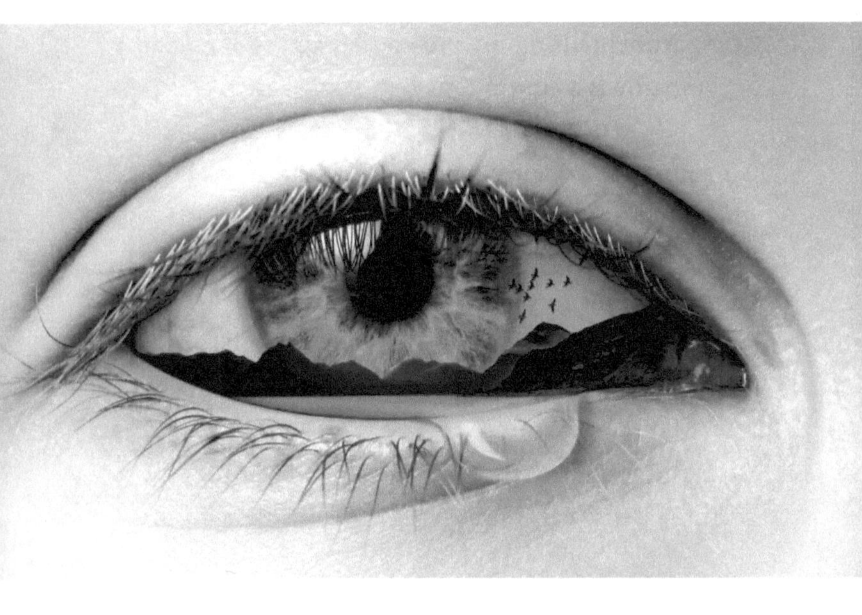

Compartmentalising my presence as an act of empathy or sympathy is a continuous fight,

For some, my presence is a sign of cowardness.. hmm.. what a sad sight.

I am the means to vent the thoughts running indiscriminately in multiple directions,
I am an expression of the most ecstatic emotions.

From the corners of the eye, sneaking out rather shy,
Truthful as a swear, I drop on the pillowcase till I dry ...

I am underrated as a means of gaining attention,
I am the honest outburst of life's unspoken dimensions.

I am a Tear.......
I am the sentiment that rediscovers the unexplored and unknown psychological layer!

The 9th

CLOUDLETS

3 65 days of work, and it was time for Amanda to take her first flight back home.

Now you'd wonder, what was so special about this one?

Amanda carried with her an invisible pandora box overflowing with experiences, learnings and the zeal of welcoming oblivious bends and caution signs along the road.

The same world that you are a part of, but Amanda viewed it from a different lens. A lens that made her see infinite opportunities, solidifying her belief in the call of the Universe. There was renewed hope, the vibrancy of the colourful journey and the path lit with lanterns of aspirations.

Cotton balls spread across the sky,
The not-so-little birdie, enabling the dreams to
effortlessly fly..

The view of the trees, the roads, playing hide and seek
through the gaps,
The kids waving up to the sky as the birdie flies through
the dots plotted on the maps..

Unknown people, similar aspirations,
Unknown journey, similar destinations.

10,800 frames, the eyes capturing them every second,
The constant gazing out of the window, inadvertently
flipping through the chapters of the past decade..

The take-off, the landing and the journey in between,
The sacrifice, the reward and the effort
intertwined..

Inching closer to the destination temporarily etched on
the map of life,
A step ahead in the direction, another honest attempt to
strive..

Touching down, being the character of the currently
streaming role play,
Awaiting a new play, the character is the one
here to stay.

The 10th

HUMANE

While on the journey back to the pavilion, her workplace, Amanda sat comfortably in the aeroplane, ready to take off.

The boarding got completed, and the aeroplane took off – with that, took off – dreams, hopes, and emotions – varied for different people onboard.

A boy, almost similar age to Amanda's, sat next to her on the flight. While Amanda was engrossed in gazing at the beauty of the sky outside, lost in her thoughts, there was turbulence, and the First Officer made his Precautionary Announcements.

She looked to the *left* only to figure out that all was not *right*.

She was perplexed..

He looked at his phone, teary-eyed, lost in thoughts. The next minute, he wiped his tears, and the poker face expression took over.

So much within, yet nothing on the face, he sat there – blank, yet the slate full, the heart drenched, yet the eyes dry.

Cannot express being the usual norm,

Crumbling within, not a sight of the humane form.

Amanda was baffled!

The sheer pressure of fake portrayal of the real self isn't sustainable, she believed.

Here's Amanda's unabashed description of how she felt about Mr Anonymous and his non-portrayal of his original self.

Stressed!
But can't express!

A high tide of emotions hits the shore,
Morale, on the verge of stepping out of the door.

The poker face look,
While around him, the glass of aspirations broke.

Mounting expectations,
The inevitable burden of relations,
Explicitly impediments his progress
Implicitly chaining his success.

Why isn't it normal to break down?
Why isn't it conventional to sometimes frown?

Who defined this 'abnormalcy' as normal?
Who sets unrealistic expectations from a mortal?

Re-set
Re-buffer
Re-invent

It's only human to express,
Emotions – Sometimes exhibiting happiness, other
times in distress..
It's only human to have highs and lows,
Teary eyes, choked throat and messed-up toes..

It's only human to have an emotional breakdown,
Falling apart, helpless, a Joker frown..

It's only human to give up momentarily,
Hopeless, dejected, down on one knee..

It's only human to break the shackles of societal
constraints,
Blurry, abstract sketch, hands still stained..

Once in a while, agreeing to loosen the reign,
Watching the world through the half-frosted window
pane..
It's only human to be humane!

The 11th

WIND

It was business as usual for Amanda. She finished her work and was heading back home from her workplace.

The raindrops pitter-pattered on the windshield of the car and knocked on the windowpane slightly.

Driving through the winding roads, the headlights of vehicles reflecting against the droplets, a plethora of thoughts captured the brain cells.

What started as a routine journey back home turned out to be a misty evening fogged in emotional nostalgia of faintly etched lullabies, settling uncertainties and undeciphered melodies.

Reaching home, Amanda rushed to the balcony. The priceless sight of the drops swinging on the leaves, the Hibiscus waving towards her, dancing to the tune of the breeze.

Blissful!

As the aroma of the brew intoxicated the room, the cerebral cells brewed a thought-provoking puzzle. The puzzle had pieces of experiences separated yet intertwined, distinct yet similar.

As she sipped her favourite French press brew, she penned down her emotions, rawness re-defined.

Cool breeze.
Dark grumbling clouds,
Raindrops merging into the puddle of water,
The air ripe with the smell of the first few drops
hugging the dry land!

Coz..
Rain is nostalgic.
Rain is magical,
Rain is an unheard melody,
Rain is a feeling of eternal bliss!

Oh yes! The monsoon wind beckons!

Was it just me who felt like floating on the lifeboat?
Thoughts dancing effortlessly like the waves of the
ocean.
Or the winds, the raindrops, and the sky played a
harmony as they met and sang a melodious lullaby..

Coz..
The monsoon rains are,
An emotion which is felt through the soul,
An emotion soothing the inner core,
An emotion calming the restlessness behind the other
side of the slightly bolted door,
An emotion settling down the unsettled, faintly known
fear,
An emotion nurturing new thoughts budding like
saplings, so pure!!

The 12th

TABOO?

The chirping of the birds, and the whispering of the trees outside Amanda's bedside window, wished her as she opened her morning eyes and looked outside.

While on her usual run, she overheard a few fellow society women talk, and emptiness took over her mind.

'How difficult is it for women to freely even purchase a pack of sanitary napkins from the shopkeeper to the fellow shopper? Everyone typically has prejudice towards the woman,' said the lady in blue.

'I need to think twice and control my pre-menstrual mood swings at work and at home even though it's not something I have control over' mentioned the other while leaning against the wall.

Amanda went into a flashback and recalled how at home, until a few years back, it was uncomfortable to talk on this subject or even let the advertisement play in its totality.

'Gasp, I feel choked!'

'This is unworthy of support.'

She shut her eyes in anguish and sighed.

'How cerebrally suffocating it is to discuss the involuntary reactions during the day.'

'Till when will a woman feel uncomfortable to get something which is her basic right to comfort and hygiene?'

These thoughts raced through Amanda's subliminal space, so she scribbled on her favourite diary.

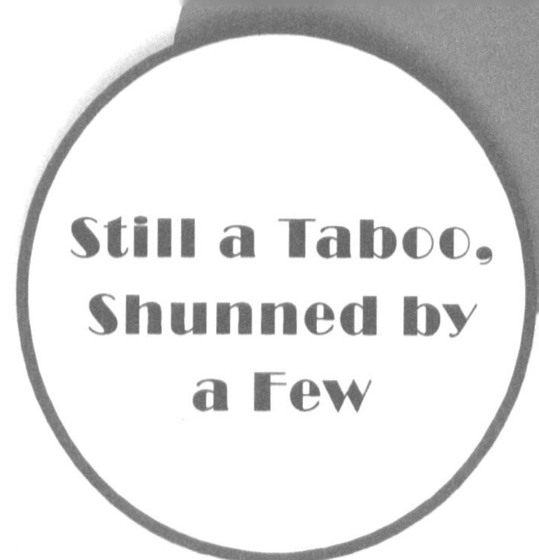

Wrapped in a newspaper,
Wrapped in a dark-coloured plastic bag.

My existence is essential,
My presence on the medical shop's shelf is,
unfortunately, uncomfortable.

The unspoken current of discomfort to discuss my
requirement has been evident,
These ideally 'not so awkward' but in reality 'oh so
awkward' discussions across homes and arenas have been
prevalent.

Switching television channels when advertisements
about me are aired,
Phew! This sight – made me sigh in despair.

Why am I such a topic of discussion and contemplation?
Why do thoughts run a mock just to move me from the
shelf to the shopping bag?

I am a pack that relieves a bleeding woman in a state of
discomfort,
I am a pack which is a constant part of the most stylish
jute tote.

Then,
How can purchasing something which is comforting be
an act of embarrassment?
How can taking a menstrual leave be so suffocatingly
difficult in this microenvironment.

It's time we liberate our actions and not memes,
It's time we do not let our fellow beings feel bereaved.
It's been a while we accepted the usual as a usual,
Instead of incessantly discussing it like a classic musical.

The 13th

BEHIND-THE-SCENES

A week went by, and it was Promotions Day in the organization!

Energized, filled with enthusiasm and zeal, everyone started to move towards the glass covered atrium.

'Wow!' exclaimed Bob, as he looked at the backdrop in the peristyle while adjusting his tie.

Mumbles and chatters filled the room as we waited for the celebrations to begin. Some of Amanda's teammates were getting promoted, and there was so much excitement in the air that evening.

The keynote speaker shares her thoughts, and the professionals celebrate their milestone achievements. It was an atmosphere filled with fun and frolic, congratulatory wishes, overwhelmingly overflowing emotions and celebratory dance.

'What an evening it was!' Bob told his group of colleagues. Just as he was saying this, his cell phone rang. It was his father. Amanda could figure out the discomfort in his voice while he spoke. She kept quiet and moved a step away from him, allowing him to talk at ease.

A few minutes later, the office commute started to line up, and as per the areas designated, they all started to disperse and head to their respective transport.

Seated in the backseat of the office cab, on the way home, a bittersweet thought went flashed Amanda's mind.

We all celebrate the result but have you ever wondered what happened 'Behind the Scenes' to reach this milestone.

Does appreciating the end suffice, or should the journey be given the focus of the lens as well?

Here's what she wrote about this while she sat comfortably in her writing zone, the table lamp tilting towards her wishfully waving.

Ever wondered if the buildings represent merely an
ensemble of stones?
Ever wondered if the cruelty behind beauty is seldom
known.
The monuments are intricately carved,
The dusty, barely hung board reading 'behind the
scenes' prohibiting the peek-a-boo beyond the wires still
barbed.

Countless sacrifices,
Oh, the fire and ice!
Appreciating the end, does that suffice?

Of fairy tales and folklore,
Unveiling the untold story bolted behind the closed
door.

The scent of the rain and iron,
The panic-stricken siren.
The swords and clothes depict a story,
From the blooming flowers to the battlefield and fury.

Truth be told, the cover doesn't depict what the book
has in store,
No wonder I get pulled inadvertently toward the
bookstore.

An attempt to peep beyond the superficial premise,
The hardships, the toil, the unsettling dice.

Someone famous today but ultimately charred,
Memories of him, sometimes decorated, sometimes
scarred.

Painting the picture slightly true, slightly imaginary,
Rolling down the car's window, the world on the other
side still blurry.

Prima facie is sadly the usually acceptable norm,
The blissful rains, though, still get invited by the
prefixed storm.

The 14ᵗʰ

WISH

The thought that she penned down lingered in her mind for a while.

While the rest of the week was 'Work as Usual' for Amanda, the weekend, this time, meant a mini-reunion with her college mates after almost a year and a half.

'A Saturday well spent after so long,' she thought while sitting near the bonfire with her friends at the resort situated on the outskirts of the city.

Carefree, singing to their heart's contentment, dancing like there is no tomorrow, laughing as if no one is watching.

It was such a profuse experience to witness this spectacle.

'I wish I could go back to the times when Prejudice and Pretentiousness were mere words in the dictionary,' said Marylin while munching on some popcorn as she thought about the 'good old college days.'

After heading back to her dome tent that night, she sighed aloud – I Wish!

And here's what she wrote on it …

I wish..

I wish.. We could go back in time,
I wish we could recite, with actions, our favourite
nursery rhyme.

I wish we could laugh without being judged,
I wish we could celebrate achievements and not hold a
grudge.

I wish each milestone could be celebrated upon,
I wish we didn't look aimlessly at dusk and dawn.

I wish we checked in, on each other, with genuine
care,
I wish social media handles weren't the only medium of
interaction with the other side of the hemisphere.

I wish we ran carefree along the beachside,
I wish we could shout out loud looking at our favourite
water slide.

I wish rollercoaster rides were only a part of the
entertainment park,
I wish there was always hope, a spark ... Beyond the
dark,
I wish phone calls were still a reality,
I wish we still understood the relevance of the word
'congeniality'.

I wish we could go back in time and smile like silly,
I wish life was a book-solving catastrophe,

I wish life was a treasure hunt,
I wish the tides of anxiety settled at the waterfront.

I wish...!
I wish!
I wish!

**I wish.. The wishes wished through the
shooting star,
Tunes of which are hummed beautifully, strummed
out of the hope's guitar.**

The 15th

CONNECT

It had been a week since Amanda and her team had welcomed a new team member, 'Jamie.'

Jamie and Amanda got out of the meeting room post a 3-hour long meeting, exhausted, looked at each other and simultaneously uttered, 'Coffee?'

And an instantaneous round of laughter followed.

Getting their Cappuccino and Americano, they returned to their workstations.

Sitting, unlocking his laptop, Jamie recalled the journey from the initial icebreaker conversation to laughter sessions and chit-chats and wondered how they connected to a different level.

While Amanda inadvertently smiled while working, thinking of the Unspoken Connect, transcending the boundaries of formalities and awkwardness towards comfort and effortlessness.

Would you imagine what happened next?

Raindrops started to lash the windowpane ...

The dream bubble gained shape, and Amanda started penning down her thoughts ...

The Unspoken Connect

The unspoken connect between dusk and dawn,
The dew drops hug the grass on the front lawn.
The toad's croak, the owl's hoot,
Watching the darkness dilute.
Strokes of greys,
Paving the way for a new day.

Numbness-soaked eyes, wishing, watching the shooting
star,
Innocence-stricken, heartfelt wishes scribbled and added
to the prettiest jar.

On another day..
At the break of dawn,
Sunflowers bloomed.
A new story weaved through hope's loom.
Sunlight sneaked through the cracks of the dusty door,
The waves of happiness lashed the emotional seashore.

Life – playing the tune unheard,
Alternating steps, the path implicitly blurred.
Scribbling on the life's book each day,
Writing and re-writing based on the experiential array.

The 16th

BOUTIQUE

Bittersweet feelings taking over the cerebral space, she smiled subtly, getting reminded of the gestures extended by Jamie.

Small talks, pointless conversations, laughing over jokes, and working together, became the usual chore.

Swamped with work and implicitly daydreaming in between.

Amanda's life portrait had fresh splashes of pastel colours, making it more vibrant and artistic.

Dusting off her knees, she stood up, her dreams transforming from larva to a beautiful butterfly, her ambitions reaching the farthermost star in the coarsely painted sky.

Beautifying her Life's boutique in a manner redefined, she set on a journey with grit and emotions intertwined.

Stars, which sparkle like diamonds in the night,
Paving the way to the morning light.

The constellations and their patterns,
Pitch dark night and the flickering flame of the
lanterns.

The autumn leaves waving goodbye to the summers,
Confidence paves its way through the path of stumbles
and bummers.

The storm and the rain,
Snowflakes knocking on the windowpane
The smile of determination to achieve, overpowering
the pain.

The larva transforms into a butterfly,
Ambitions unlocking the cage to fly..

The stream danced over the pebbles..
In an attempt to explore its destination, reaching
unimaginable levels,
Re-energizing self to lift from the shambles,
Decoding the message lost in the scramble.

Transforming from introspection to
self-exploration,
Simplifying the mental complication.

From lows to Highs,
Calming the high tides,
Days of anguish and despair ... Sigh!
Yet, the sun rays sneaking through the
overcast sky.

When the subliminal mind and the active thoughts play
hide and seek in the attic,
Being your own critique,
Contemplating between capability and self-belief,
Shunning the disbelief
Reminding self of the walk towards the
winning streak,
In the end, Beautifying life's boutique!!

The 17th

AESTHETIC

$\mathbf{P}$art of the beautification involved her to artistically transform her room.

While strumming the tune of John Denver's 'Country Roads, take me Home,' she smiled dreamily, thinking about the dream catcher, wind chime, and cosy low-lying seating space. Amanda had already started assembling the pieces of the puzzle in her thoughts.

Sipping a cup of coffee minutes later, crouching in one corner of the room, she exclaimed, "Umm, Let's replace the usual lights with filament bulbs?"

Carrying that thought along, stacking her favourite collection of books on the bookshelf and Jenga on the other end, the aesthetics-driven side of Amanda started to emerge and unfold …

Filament bulbs swaying to the song of the breeze,
The sight of rustic bookshelves got back memories and
made the brain freeze,
The guitar resting effortlessly against the wall,
Pictionary and Jenga invariably catch the attention of all,
Chitter chatter of a few making it spirited,
The old-school charm and instrumental music add to
the ambience..

She stood there captivated by the serenity of the
environment,
Mentally liberated than being confined to the four walls
of the apartment.

Some places exude positivity, and their existence a
blessing,
Your inner self unknowingly gets magnetized toward
your calling ...
That's when the mind, heart, and soul are felt leisurely
strolling ...

The 18th

VAGABOND

Excited, Amanda called Jamie and showed him the transformed room.

Jamie, awestruck looking at the efforts, exclaimed, 'Wow! Now that's a distinct level of creativity.'

They spoke for hours that evening, discussing what went 'behind the scenes' to reach the finish line for the room décor, random laughter sessions, and silly small talk.

Their bond was stronger than before, and their thoughts synced like never before. Amanda and Jamie's bond had a distinct flair of authenticity and wittiness.

They, being together at any place, meant the room would echo with letters of laughter and waves of joy.

Ordering their favourite meals, discussing travel destinations through the traveller's lens, assuring the other in times of self-doubt, and celebrating every single step of life, their journey, which, even though it had just begun, was surely unmatched.

Liking you just like you do,
You, being the one always on the mind,
Towards you, involuntarily inclined..

Every ring of the phone, hoping it is yours,
Notes, written for you, overflowing out of the
drawers..

To travel with you is a virtue,
One hand out of the window,
Of destination-- no clue!

To conversations, to twilight hues,
Aesthetically pleasing views..

Liking you just like you do,
I don't talk about it, and neither do you..

Hoping we are being afraid of the truth,
But paving the path through the same route..

Ignoring un-spelt apprehension,
Giving the unnamed emotion a new dimension.

This is just the start of Amanda's journey. How she describes her *'Little Joys of Life'* is in the making and will be on your bookshelf soon. Hoping you join Amanda's next phase of life and enjoy traversing this expedition with her……

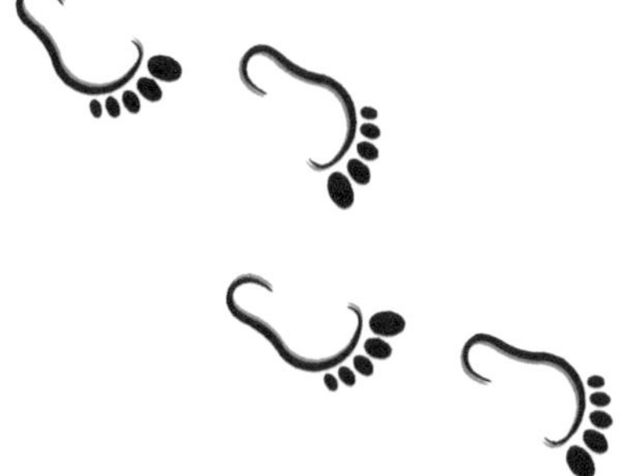